Jessica Souhami studied textile design at the
Central School of Art and Design. For several years she
ran Mme Souhami & Co., a travelling shadow puppet company,
performing playground songs, magical pieces and folk tales from many cultures.
The Leopard's Drum is an adaptation of one of the company's most successful productions.
Jessica Souhami works in collaboration with book designer Paul McAlinden. Their other titles for
Frances Lincoln include: *Old MacDonald*, which was chosen as one of Child Education's
Best Books of 1996, *Rama and the Demon King*, which has been selected for the
National Literacy Association Guide to Literary Resources, *Silly Rhymes:*
One Potato, Two Potato and *Mother Caught a Flea*, *The Black Geese*,
retold by Alison Lurie, and *No Dinner!*

To Gulzar Kanji

An Ancient Tale from India

Rama and the Demon King

Retold and illustrated by Jessica Souhami

FRANCES LINCOLN

This is the story of a brave and good prince called Rama,
who should have been the happiest of men.

After all, he was the King's favourite son. He had a
dear wife called Sita, and he had the best of friends in his
brother, Lakshman.

And all the people in the kingdom loved him.

Well, all but one...
and that was his jealous stepmother.

She HATED Rama.

And she planned to get rid of him forever.

So she set a trap...

Rama's wicked stepmother went to the King.

"Long ago," she said, "I saved your life and you promised to grant me any wish. Now I want you to send Rama into the forest for fourteen years."

The King was horrified. The forest was full of terrible demons. But what could he do?

A king MUST keep his promise.

With a broken heart, he sent Rama away.

But Sita and Lakshman would not let Rama go alone. So that very day, all three left the palace to face the dangers of the forest together.

In the forest, news of Rama's exile spread fast.

The demons hated anyone good and they were spoiling for a fight. As soon as Rama, Sita and Lakshman appeared, the demons attacked them gleefully.

But both princes were brilliant fighters. They fought back bravely and killed thousands of demons until at last there was peace in the forest.

Rama, Sita and Lakshman built a house, gathered fruit and berries for food and lived a quiet and simple life among the forest animals.

BUT it was not to last.

Far away, in a magnificent palace on the island of Lanka, lived Ravana, the ten-headed king of all the demons.

He was evil and proud.

"No one can defeat me," he boasted. "No one is stronger than me. No one is more cunning. No one knows as much magic."

He smiled ten horrible smiles.

One day, a messenger arrived from India and told Ravana how Rama and Lakshman had killed thousands of his demons.

"WHAAAAT!" his ten mouths screeched.

And he quivered with rage.

Ravana leapt into his magic chariot and flew to India. There he hid in a tree, ready to pounce on Rama and Lakshman.

But when he caught sight of Sita he stopped short, dazzled by her beauty.

"She must be my queen!" he muttered. "I'll steal her from Rama and leave him broken-hearted. Serve him right for killing my demons!"

And his ten brains buzzed with evil schemes.

This is what Ravana did.

He sent a magic deer into the forest, a golden creature which enchanted Sita. But whenever she tried to stroke it, it moved just out of reach.

Rama offered to catch it for her.

"Lakshman," he said, "look after Sita while I'm gone. There may still be demons about."

And he followed the deer until they both disappeared from view.

All was quiet.

Suddenly, Sita and Lakshman heard a cry.

"Help me! Help me, Lakshman!"

It sounded just like Rama.

Now, what should Lakshman do?

He could not look for Rama. He had to protect Sita.

But Sita said, "Leave me, Lakshman, and rescue Rama.
I'm safe here. Hurry!"

Then Lakshman ran as fast as he could towards the voice.

But, of course, it was not Rama calling.

It was a fiendish trick of Ravana's.

And now Sita was alone.

Wicked Ravana swooped down and carried her off in his magic chariot.

Meanwhile, Lakshman found Rama unhurt. With horror, the brothers realised they had been tricked.

They raced back to Sita.

But she was gone.

Rama was desolate.

The two brothers looked all over India for Sita.
Their search seemed hopeless.

Then, one day, they came to the land of the monkeys.
There they met Hanuman, the leader of the monkey army,
and told him their story.

"Ravana has taken Sita," said Hanuman. "We saw them
flying towards his palace on the island of Lanka."

"But how can we reach her?" asked Rama. "The sea round
Lanka is full of monsters."

"I think I can help you," said Hanuman. "My father is Vayu, the Wind God, and so I can fly like the wind! I will find Sita for you."

Rama and Lakshman were astonished.

"Take my ring," said Rama. "When you find Sita, give it to her so she will know I sent you. Good luck."

And Hanuman flew across the treacherous sea to Lanka.

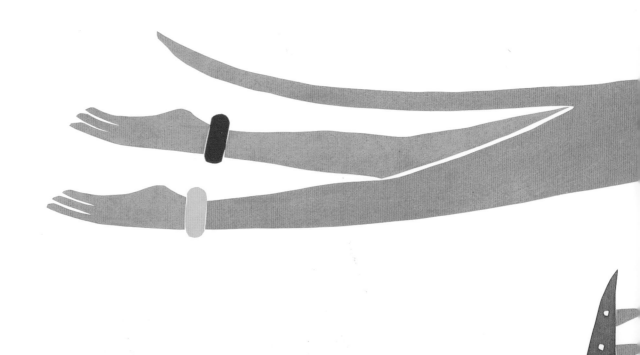

Hanuman found Sita imprisoned in Ravana's garden.

He gave her Rama's ring.

"I'm so glad to see you," she cried. "I've refused to become Ravana's queen. If I don't change my mind, he says he will chop me into little pieces and eat me up for breakfast!"

"Be brave, Sita," whispered Hanuman. "We will be back for you soon."

Hanuman returned to Rama with his news, and the monkey army prepared for battle.

They began by building an amazing bridge which stretched right across the sea from India to Lanka.

Then the army, led by Rama, Lakshman and Hanuman, marched across it!

Ravana's demon army was waiting for them on Lanka.

A terrible battle began.

The demons tried all their evil tricks.

Some used magic arrows that turned into poisonous snakes. Others became invisible, so that the monkeys only saw a sea of whirling weapons. There were giant demons with enormous strength and demons who could move at the speed of light.

But Rama, Lakshman and the monkey army stood firm and, after many days of fierce fighting, the demons were defeated.

BUT THEN...

Ravana appeared, his twenty eyes blazing.

"Ha, Rama!" he sneered. "You know you cannot beat ME!"

Rama was silent. He slowly raised his bow and released a magic arrow.

It found its own way to Ravana. It pierced his evil body. Ravana was DEAD.

Rama and Sita were reunited and they returned to India. Sadness overshadowed the land, for Rama's father had died of grief on the day they left the palace. But now the people rejoiced that Rama was home.

Rama was made king, with Sita his queen, and Lakshman and Hanuman at his side.

The celebrations lasted for a whole month. Even the stepmother who had plotted against Rama was invited.

Rama ruled wisely and well.

The land became fruitful, and at last the kingdom was free from all evil.

The story of Rama, who rescues his wife, Sita, from
the Demon King, has been told in India for thousands of years
and is said to confer a blessing on all who hear it.

The legend may have been based on historical fact.
It was passed from person to person until, in about 400 B.C.,
the poet Valmiki wrote the *Ramayana*. Almost every regional language
in India has its own version, and the story has spread throughout
south-east Asia. Heroic saga, love story and symbolic account
of the battle between good and evil, the *Ramayana* has
inspired countless works of art and literature.

Rama and the Demon King copyright © Frances Lincoln Limited 1997
Text, illustrations and design copyright © Jessica Souhami and Paul McAlinden 1997

First published in Great Britain in 1997 by
Frances Lincoln Limited, 4 Torriano Mews
Torriano Avenue, London NW5 2RZ

British Library Cataloguing in Publication Data available on request

ISBN hardback 0-7112-1111-6
ISBN paperback 0-7112-1158-2

Set in Monotype News Plantin

Printed in Hong Kong

5 7 9 8 6

MORE PICTURE BOOKS IN PAPERBACK
BY JESSICA SOUHAMI

The Leopard's Drum
Jessica Souhami

How a very small tortoise outwits a boastful leopard to capture his drum is
dramatically retold in this traditional Asante tale from West Africa.
Jessica Souhami has adapted her own shadow puppet images to create bold illustrations.

Suitable for National Curriculum English – Reading, Key Stage 2
Scottish Guidelines English Language – Reading, Level B

ISBN 0-7112-0907-3

No Dinner!
Jessica Souhami

In this popular Southern Asian story, an old woman doesn't know how she will
ever get home safely with a hungry wolf, a hungry bear and a hungry tiger waiting
for her on the way. Then her granddaughter has an idea…

Suitable for National Curriculum English – Reading, Key Stage 1
Scottish Guidelines English Language – Reading, Levels A and B

ISBN 0-7112-1459-X

The Black Geese
A Baba Yaga Folktale from Russia
Retold by Alison Lurie
Illustrated by Jessica Souhami

Elena will need all her courage and a kind heart, as well as the help of three magic gifts,
if she is to save her baby brother from the terrible witch Baba Yaga.

Suitable for National Curriculum English – Reading, Key Stages 1 and 2
Scottish Guidelines English Language – Reading, Levels A and B

ISBN 0-7112-1444-1

Frances Lincoln titles are available from all good bookshops.